DC COMICS™
SUPER HEROES

SUPERMAN

PRANKSTER
OF PRIME TIME

WRITTEN BY
MARTIN PASKO

ILLUSTRATED BY
RICK BURCHETT AND
LEE LOUGHRIDGE

SUPERMAN CREATED BY
JERRY SIEGEL AND
~~JOE~~ SHUSTER

D0522943

04299211

First published in this format in 2014 by Curious Fox,
an imprint of Capstone Global Library Limited,
7 Pilgrim Street, London, EC4V 6LB
– Registered company number: 6695582

www.curious-fox.com
The moral rights of the proprietor have been asserted.

CAPG33553

Art Director: Bob Lentz
Designers: Hilary Wacholz and Steve Mead
Production Controller: Helen McCreath
Editors: Vaarunika Dharmapala, Dan Nunn and Holly Beaumont
Originated by Capstone Global Library Ltd
Printed and bound in China by Leo Paper Group

ISBN 978 1 78202 149 0
18 17 16 15 14
10 9 8 7 6 5 4 3 2 1

A CIP catalogue record for this book is available
from the British Library.

CONTENTS

CHAPTER 1

CAR TROUBLE

WHOOOOSH! Superman soared above the city of Metropolis. He was flying overhead on his usual patrol, looking down with his super-vision. This superpower allowed him to see faraway objects as though they were just a few metres away.

As he scanned the city with his X-ray vision, he spotted three suspicious men at a luxury car dealership. Each of them was trying to break into an expensive car. One was picking the lock of a gigantic four-wheel drive car. Another had smashed the window of a convertible.

The third crook was already behind the wheel of a German sports car with shiny wheel rims and a custom paint job.

Superman landed inside the dealership. Immediately, all three of the burglars panicked. They ran for the door.

Without hesitating, the Man of Steel stomped his foot on the floor. **THUD!** The force of the stomp made the whole building shake. **RUMMMMMMMMMMMBLE!** The crooks tripped and fell before they could reach the exit.

As the men struggled to their feet, Superman grabbed hold of the four-wheel drive. He opened the back doors and then effortlessly pushed the car towards them.

SKREEE-EEE-EEECH!

The open boot of the big car swallowed two of the crooks, and then slid against the wall. Neither of the men were hurt, but now they were trapped!

Superman made sure they could not escape by melting the locks with his heat vision. *BZZT!*

Meanwhile, the third burglar had released the emergency brake on another car. It was rolling towards a chair in the corner of the showroom. Just then, Superman noticed a security guard sitting in the chair! The crooks had tied him up with plastic cord and put tape over his mouth.

Superman leapt between the guard and the car, gently stopping it with his super-strong hands.

While Superman had been saving the guard, the third crook had vanished from sight.

The Man of Steel ripped through the heavy cord that bound the guard. **SNAP!** The plastic split apart as though it were an old rubber band.

Superman gently removed the tape from the man's mouth. "Are you okay?" asked the Man of Steel.

"I think so," the guard replied. "Thanks, Superman!"

BARROOOOOMME The sound of a siren meant the police had arrived.

The superhero dragged the big car away from the wall. The two crooks shot Superman a nervous glance and stayed put inside the car's boot.

The police swarmed into the showroom, led by Lieutenant Dawn Valens.

She glanced inside the car and smiled. "You always come up with such interesting ways of catching criminals, Superman," she said.

"I'm afraid the third criminal escaped," Superman told her. "I can't find any trace of him."

"Don't worry, Superman," Lieutenant Valens said. "We'll catch him eventually."

Superman scanned the floor with his X-ray vision. In a corner, he saw a hole that the crooks must have dug. A tunnel beneath the building led to its basement. The burglars had entered the dealership from underground! Superman immediately told the police about the tunnel.

Then, in the blink of an eye, Superman moved the vehicles back into place and repaired the damage done to the car's locks.

He flew to the *Daily Planet* building. Suddenly, his super-hearing picked up an excited voice on a television, talking about a practical joke. It was a voice he had hoped he would never hear ever again. A voice that meant just one thing – trouble!

CHAPTER 2

GOTCHA!

Superman landed on the *Daily Planet* building's rooftop. He stepped into the stairwell to change into his Clark Kent clothes. He kept his X-ray vision and super-hearing trained on the television.

A small crowd stood around one of the television screens normally tuned in to news channels. Clark's friends, reporter Lois Lane, and the *Daily Planet*'s young photographer, Jimmy Olsen, were there. They were watching *Gotcha!*

Gotcha! was the most successful new

reality programme on television. It showed people pulling pranks on each other. The host was a hot new star named Alex Ryan.

Suddenly, editor-in-chief Perry White started yelling. "What are you people doing?" he shouted. "It certainly doesn't look like work!" The reporters scurried back to their desks. Only Jimmy and Lois remained in front of the television.

"Look at this, Chief!" Jimmy said, pointing to the television.

The screen showed a corner shop that was in a total mess. Customers were slipping and sliding on the floor, which was covered in a deep puddle of bright red slush. A boy behind the counter was trying to turn off the "Shmushie" drink machine, but the button would not work.

Nothing could stop the streams of Shmushie that kept oozing on to the floor, over the countertops, everywhere!

"This programme rocks!" Jimmy said, laughing. "Alex Ryan is a genius!"

"You mean all this is being done on purpose?" asked Perry White.

"Of course," Jimmy said. "Kids audition for the programme. If they get chosen, they get to play pranks on their friends on TV!"

The face of Alex Ryan appeared on the screen. He continued explaining what was happening in the shop.

"Darren's co-workers got tired of him leaving a mess every time he made a Shmushie," Ryan said. "So, they rigged the machine to make the biggest mess of all! Perhaps he's learned his lesson now!"

"That's hilarious!" Jimmy said, letting out another laugh. "Best host ever!"

Lois thought that Ryan's spiky hair, goatee and bright white teeth seemed a little *too* perfect. "This Alex Ryan looks kind of familiar," she said. "And why's he talking so strangely?"

Clark stepped out of the room. He was trying to focus on something. His super-hearing was able to identify suspects from recordings, even when they tried to disguise their voices. Clark could tell that Ryan was using a fake voice.

In the news room, Perry White switched off the TV set and stomped back into his office. "Back to work!" he shouted.

THUD! The walls shook as the door slammed behind him.

Lois turned to see Clark Kent come back into the room. "I was just talking to Superman," Clark said. "You were right about Alex Ryan, Lois. Superman thinks he's really Oswald Loomis in disguise."

Lois's eyes widened. "You mean Superman's old enemy, the Prankster?" she asked.

"That's right," said Clark. "He was recently released from jail."

Jimmy chuckled. "Then he's found the perfect way to use his skills. Now he can play pranks on people and get paid for it!"

Clark was not so sure. "If Loomis really wanted to stay on the right side of the law, he would have done it long ago," he said.

Jimmy knew what Clark meant. Oswald Loomis was not just mean, he was crazy.

He could not stop himself from pulling pranks. Not even psychiatrists could help him. What was worse – his pranks almost always led to people getting hurt.

Lois shook her head. "That doesn't prove he's up to something," she said. "We need hard evidence."

"You know," Jimmy said, "the programme uses kids my age. This is my chance to show the Chief that I can do more than just snap photos!"

"What do you mean?" Lois asked, looking confused.

"I'm going to be an investigative reporter just like you two," Jimmy said excitedly. "I'm going undercover!"

"Wait, Jimmy," Clark said. "That's too dangerous. You don't have any training!"

But it was too late. Jimmy had run out of the room before anyone could stop him.

Clark and Lois exchanged nervous glances. Now, they had something more than just the Prankster to be worried about!

CHAPTER 3

MEET BART ALTON

In the production offices of *Gotcha! Studios*, a boy with black hair and glasses was doing a magic trick. He made a coin disappear from the palm of his hand while a camera operator taped it. Alex Ryan stood nearby, watching very closely.

"You've got talent, Bart," said Kayla, the programme's producer. "And you look great on camera." She was watching him on a screen and taking notes.

Bart Alton, of course, was really James Bartholomew Olsen in disguise.

Jimmy was wearing a black wig and a pair of fake glasses to complete his disguise.

Kayla dismissed the camera operator, then turned to Jimmy. "Be back here tomorrow morning at ten," she said. "We'll use you for one of our programmes."

Jimmy let out a cheer of victory. "I can't wait!" he shouted. He grabbed his jacket off the back of a chair and dashed off. "See you tomorrow," he said, closing the door behind him.

Out in the empty corridor, he saw a sign for the exit. Instead, he went in the opposite direction. The sight of a vent on the wall had given him an idea.

Back in the studio, Ryan was standing just behind the chair where Jimmy had hung his jacket during his audition.

"Let's use him for the car prank," Kayla said, looking up from her notes. She noticed Ryan was holding something in his hand.

"Not so fast," Ryan said, but his voice had suddenly changed into a high-pitched whine. "We have to do some research on that kid." He stepped out into the corridor, and led Kayla to his private office.

There, he closed the door behind Kayla and held up the object he had found. It was a *Daily Planet* notepad that he had stolen from Jimmy's jacket. "He had this in his pocket," Ryan said. "I think he's hiding something."

Kayla tried not to laugh as Ryan pulled off his wig and fake beard. *He looks so ridiculous without his disguise*, she thought. *I don't know why he doesn't just keep it on all the time!*

Alex then removed his false teeth, revealing himself as the gap-toothed Oswald Loomis.

"Hey, Prankie," said Kayla with a laugh. "You look much better with the wig and teeth."

"I told you not to call me that!" Loomis shouted. Before he could go on, there was a knock at the glass door. It was the burglar from the car dealership, the one that had got away. Grinning, the Prankster opened it and reached out to shake the man's hand. The thief took a step back and shook his head.

"Oh no, you don't, Prankster!" said the burglar. "The last time we shook hands, I got an electric shock! I won't fall for that trick again."

Loomis held up his hands. "Relax, Pug," he said. "See? No buzzer! Come on, shake!"

Pug shrugged. He extended his arm and shook the Prankster's hand.

SPLASH! Instead of an electric shock, he got a face full of water from the Prankster's squirt gun. Kayla giggled as Pug wiped off his face.

"Thanks," Pug said angrily. "Now I don't feel so bad about telling you that I don't have your money."

No one in the room noticed it, but above their heads, Jimmy Olsen was listening. He had removed the screw from the grate of the vent, and squeezed inside. Then, he had crawled through the duct in the direction of Pug's voice.

"Not my problem," the Prankster replied. His voice was cold and menacing. "You know the rules. I had those kids dig that tunnel and install the pipe in it. They thought it was part of a prank, but it was really your entrance and escape route. For that, you owe me."

Jimmy had heard about the robbery, and he was starting to figure out what the Prankster was planning.

"All you had to do was dig a little more and cut a hole in the wall," the Prankster said. "It's not my fault you messed it up."

The Prankster shoved Pug out of the office. "You've got until noon tomorrow to come up with the cash," he snarled. "Or else…!"

CLINK CLANK!

"Did you hear something?" asked the Prankster.

"I think it came from above," said Kayla.

The Prankster looked up towards the faint noise. Jimmy held his breath. He had dropped his mobile phone, which he had been using to record the conversation.

Jimmy grabbed his phone and started crawling away as fast as he could, but the phone's light had gone out. He was in total darkness now.

ZWWWOOOOMMMM! Suddenly, Jimmy was sliding down a steeply angled vent. Then he crashed through a grate and landed with a thud in the middle of a storage room. He looked up to see walls lined with shelves of DVDs.

The DVDs were recorded episodes of *Gotcha!* Then, Jimmy caught sight of something very strange. An entire row was labelled "Not for broadcasting."

Now Jimmy was sure he had found the evidence that would prove Clark's theory.

CHAPTER 4

BART GETS THE GOODS

Back at the *Daily Planet* building, Perry, Lois, Clark and Jimmy were once again gathered around a television screen. But this time, they were watching several DVDs that Jimmy had smuggled out of the *Gotcha!* offices after everyone had left.

"I had to stay there practically all night to make sure I could escape without being seen," Jimmy said, "but it was worth it."

The show on the screen was one of the "Not for broadcasting" episodes.

The episode was about kids digging a tunnel. The victim of the prank was told that the tunnel would help him sneak under a fence to an amusement park. The trick was that it led nowhere.

"So that's how the robbers got into the car dealership," Lois said.

"Exactly," said Clark. "Lieutenant Valens told me the police found the tunnel when Pug got away. They had no idea where it came from."

Lois pointed to the monitor. "They would have known, if this show had been broadcast," she said. "People could make a connection between the crime and *Gotcha!*"

"No wonder Superman couldn't spot the third robber," Perry said. "That pipe must have been made of lead."

"Superman's X-ray vision wouldn't have been able to see through it," Jimmy said. "You'll have to figure out the rest of it without me. I've got to get back to the studio."

"Jimmy," Lois said worriedly, "you came this close to being caught in that air duct. You've done some great work so far, but –"

Jimmy cut her off. "Yes, Ms Lane," he said, flashing a smile. "And if I ever need another mother, I'll know where to find you!" With that, he dashed out of the office before anyone could say another word.

Perry shook his head. "Maybe that kid's got what it takes, after all," he said. Clark and Lois looked surprised. "But if you tell him I said so, you're fired."

"No worries, Perry," Lois said.

"The kids don't commit any crimes," Lois said. "They help set them up."

Suddenly, the phone rang. Lois picked it up and sat down at her desk.

"That's crazy!" Perry said. "Why would anyone go to all that trouble? Why wouldn't Loomis just do the jobs himself?"

Clark smiled. "You said it yourself, Chief," he said. "Loomis is crazy. He's one of those 'theme criminals'. His crimes always have to involve a prank!"

Clark knew it was time for Superman to get involved. "If you'll excuse me, Chief," Clark said, "I have a different story to finish writing."

As Clark left, Lois put down the phone. "That was Lieutenant Valens. She wanted to thank you for the copies of those DVDs."

Lois rushed to the door. "She's on her way to the studio now with an arrest warrant," Lois added. "Let's go!"

*   *   *

By the time Lois arrived at the *Gotcha!* offices with her video camera, Superman was standing with the police in front of the empty, two-story building.

"What's going on?" asked Lois as she raced up to Superman.

"They somehow worked out that we were on to them," said Lieutenant Valens.

"I've checked out the whole place," Superman said grimly, "and it's empty."

Lois's eyes widened with worry.

"That's right, Lois," Superman said. "There's no sign of Jimmy, either."

CHAPTER 5

THE BIG BANG

The Prankster had captured Jimmy Olsen, and there was nothing he could do about it. After removing his disguise, the crook handcuffed Jimmy and put him in the back seat of his car.

Kayla was driving them down a back street in a bad part of town. They were almost at their destination, the back entrance to a run-down building.

"We saw the mess you left downstairs this morning," the Prankster snarled. "This is your chance to talk!"

"Someone has been helping themselves to our DVD collection," the Prankster said.

Jimmy said nothing. He just continued what he had been doing since the Prankster had handcuffed him. He was doing it very, very slowly, so no one would notice. He was moving his right hand towards his left.

"Somebody removed the grate over an air duct, too," the Prankster said, holding up a large screw. "But they forgot to replace all the bolts."

Jimmy winced. He had thought he had been so careful. Lois and Clark were right. Undercover work is dangerous unless you know exactly what you are doing.

"We've never had trouble like that before you came along," the Prankster screamed. "Who are you? What do you want?"

Finally Jimmy was able to reach the button on the side of his wristwatch. It made a special sound, a high-frequency distress call that only Superman could hear.

Back at the empty warehouse, Lois was busy interviewing Lieutenant Valens on her video camera.

THWOOOOMMM!!!

They turned to see Superman fly straight up in the air. They could not know, however, that the Prankster had glanced down just as Jimmy pushed the button. Now he tore the watch off Jimmy's wrist and smashed it against the car door.

The Prankster was beginning to get it. "The *Daily Planet* notepad, the watch …! You're Superman's friend, Jimmy Olsen!"

Jimmy gulped.

By now, Jimmy had been led to the open doorway of a dark warehouse. The daylight from the alley did not allow him to see much. He could barely make out piles of shipping crates and bubble wrap. There were also stacks of boxes filled with unsold novelties, like decks of marked playing cards and trick coins.

The Prankster pointed at what looked like several scattered pillows. "You've heard of whoopee cushions?"

The Prankster grinned as he took a screw out of his pocket. "Well, take a look at this!" The Prankster tossed the screw on to one of the pillows.

Ba-Doooommmm!!!

The "whoopee cushion" exploded with the force of a hand grenade!

The Prankster chuckled nastily. "Here, every day is April Fool's Day," he said. "I store all my cleverest inventions here."

Then the Prankster started blindfolding Jimmy with his handkerchief. Jimmy tried to act brave. As everything went dark, however, he knew he was in serious trouble.

*   *   *

Superman landed back at the studio. "Jimmy's signal stopped before I could track it down," he told Lois.

Lois seemed confused. "Can't you use your super-vision to find him?"

But before Superman could reply, Lois added, "In a city this size, though, where would you even start?"

"I may have an idea," Superman said.

Superman pointed to Lois's video camera, which she had been using to tape her interview. "Rewind your video, and play it again, Lois."

Lois did as Superman asked. The video had picked up the sound of Jimmy's signal. It told the Man of Steel how far away and in which direction Jimmy was. In seconds, he was rocketing towards the Metropolis warehouse district. With his super-vision, he scanned every building and shop window.

*   *   *

Meanwhile, back in the warehouse, the Prankster gave Jimmy a rough shove. The boy stumbled forward, stepping closer and closer to the exploding pillows. Between the handcuffs and the blindfold, Jimmy could barely keep his balance. He had no idea where he was going.

ZWWWOOOOMMMM!

He heard a familiar sound of rushing wind and thought the crooks had run away.

He turned in what he thought was their direction. Jimmy did not realize he was about to step on one of the explosive cushions.

Just as his foot was lowering down on top of a pillow, he felt a hand grab his ankle. Another hand gripped his wrists. **FWOOSHHHHH!** He was being lifted into the air!

"Superman!" he cried.

The Man of Steel set him down safely in the packing and shipping area, far from the deadly pillows. "Thanks!" said Jimmy, with relief.

"No problem, Jimmy," Superman said as he removed Jimmy's blindfold and handcuffs. "Or, should I call you Bart?"

Jimmy frowned. "Are you making fun of me, Superman?" he asked.

"No, not at all," Superman reassured him. "You did some great work out there. You're a natural reporter."

Jimmy smiled shyly. "Wow, thanks!" he said.

"Just promise me one thing," Superman added. "Be a little more careful next time."

When he was free of his restraints, Jimmy called the police on his mobile phone.

"Wait here, Jimmy," Superman said. "The Prankster is unpredictable, so we'll have to be cautious until the police arrive."

In the alley, the Prankster and Kayla had almost made it to their car when Superman appeared in front of them. He was standing in their path and blocking their escape. They heard the sound of approaching police sirens. Quickly, they turned and ran back to the warehouse.

Suddenly, the two crooks came running frantically back into the alley. They held their hands above their heads.

"Don't shoot, don't shoot, we give up!" they cried out to Superman. "Please don't let the police shoot us!"

Superman quickly grabbed the two criminals. As he led them away, the Man of Steel smiled from ear to ear.

"What's so funny?" The Prankster asked.

Just then, the Prankster heard the sound of sirens growing louder.

"The police haven't even arrived yet," Superman said. He nodded at Jimmy, who was standing in the doorway.

Jimmy held a sheet of plastic bubble wrap used for packing. He popped a few, giggling at the Prankster. BANG! BANG!

For once, the victim of a prank was the Prankster himself!

WHO IS THE PRANKSTER?

Oswald Loomis once led a happy, laughter-filled life as the host of a popular children's television programme. He told jokes, made kids giggle, and had plenty of cash. But when the powers that be decided to axe Oswald's show, he went crazy – and vowed to take Metropolis's citizens down with him. As the Prankster, he plays deadly gags, with only the Man of Steel standing between him and madness. The Prankster may be a clown, but he is no joke – this crazy trickster is always trying to make a fool out of the Man of Steel.

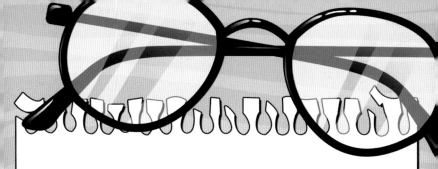

- The Prankster uses a variety of deadly gags to distract and incapacitate his victims. He created a device that makes people giggle uncontrollably so he can steal people's belongings while they are doubled over in laughter. He also uses electric buzzers and exploding whoopee cushions in his comical capers.

- Rather than commit crimes himself, the Prankster is instead paid by criminals to distract Superman with his pranks. That way, the crooks can commit crimes without the Man of Steel around to stop them.

- The Prankster once managed to trademark the English language! He then forced anyone who spoke or wrote in English to pay him by the word. Since Loomis had not broken the law, Superman could not do anything to stop him – until he found out that Oswald had bribed an official to get his patent.

- Loomis owns Uncle Oley's Sure Fire Joke Shop. It appears to be a normal magic and joke shop, but a hidden trapdoor leads to a high-tech underground base where the Prankster plans all his crimes.

Other CURIOUS FOX titles you might be interested in...

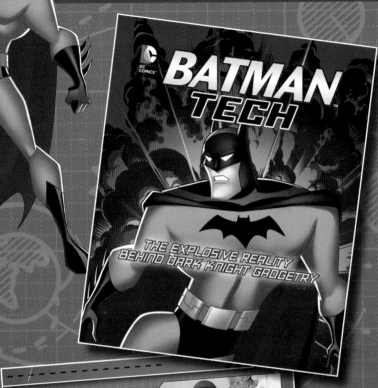

DC COMICS™

BATMAN TECH™

THE EXPLOSIVE REALITY BEHIND DARK KNIGHT GADGETRY

BODY ARMOUR

To fight crime, Batman puts himself in the line of fire. The Batsuit is the only thing that stands between him and all kinds of lethal impacts. To protect him, it includes body armour – a technology that has come a long way over the centuries.

The history of body armour spans thousands of years. Ancient tribes used animal hides and woven plant material for protection from cuts and scrapes. The ancient Romans covered their chests with metal breastplates. Full-body metal armour came into its glory by the 1400s. Medieval knights covered themselves from head to toe in metal plates to protect against sword thrusts or arrows.

Once cannons and guns were developed, traditional armour fell by the wayside. To protect from these kinds of impacts, metal armour would be too heavy to wear.

Medieval knights protected themselves with heavy metal armour.

Soldiers put on armoured bomb suits before disabling explosive devices.

But as weapons have changed, body armour has evolved too. Today soldiers and police protect themselves with either hard or soft body armour. Hard body armour is similar to the metal armour of the Middle Ages. It protects well, but is heavy and cumbersome. Soft body armour is woven out of advanced materials sewn into vests and other clothing. It is much more comfortable than wearing heavy metal plates. The most famous material used in soft body armour is Kevlar.

DC COMICS™
SUPER HEROES

Curious Fox

DC
COMICS™

SUPER
HEROES

SUPERMAN

THE DEADLY DOUBLE

LITTLE GREEN MEN

LIVEWIRE!

PRANKSTER OF PRIME TIME

METEOR OF DOOM

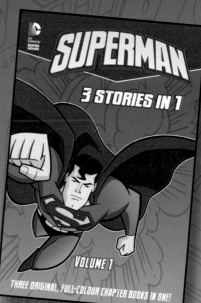

SUPERMAN

3 STORIES IN 1

VOLUME 1

THREE ORIGINAL, FULL-COLOUR CHAPTER BOOKS IN ONE!

3 STORIES IN 1

DC COMICS™
SUPER HEROES

BATMAN

SCARECROW, DOCTOR OF FEAR

THE FOG OF FEAR

MAD HATTER'S MOVIE MADNESS

THE REVENGE OF CLAYFACE

ROBIN'S FIRST FLIGHT

3 Stories in 1

Volume 1

THREE ORIGINAL, FULL-COLOUR CHAPTER BOOKS IN ONE!

3 STORIES IN 1

Curious Fox

SCOOBY-DOO! MYSTERIES

Solve a mystery with Scooby~Doo!

SCOOBY-DOO AND THE GROOVY GHOST

SCOOBY-DOO AND THE KARATE CAPER

SCOOBY-DOO AND THE SUNKEN SHIP

SCOOBY-DOO AND THE VAMPIRE'S REVENGE

For more exciting books
from brilliant authors,
follow the fox!

www.curious-fox.com

Curious
Fox